Stalking in the New Year

EMMA BRAY

CHAPTER
One

Cal

I WATCH her up on the stage, my chest squeezing painfully at the sight of her.

It's been this way for months, like I'm constantly on the verge of a heart attack every time I see her scantily clad form performing for countless eyes of men.

They're captivated by her. Just like me.

I happened to come into this bar one day after a long day at the gym, and there she was.

Up on the stage. Dancing her little heart out.

But here's the thing about her.

She's not like the other dancers.

She doesn't dance like a stripper.

She dances like a ballerina. With poise and grace. Even when she's trying to dance erotically, there's something deeper that she can't seem to get away from. There's an inherent artform to her dancing.

Of course, I know why that is. I know everything about her, though she doesn't even know I exist. I've made it my business to know.

Sexy Lexi. That's what they call her.

She's a tiny thing with the longest red hair I've ever seen and emerald green eyes that are enough to knock the wind out of a man. That hair brushes the top of her ass and sways sensually around her hips with every movement. And she might be little, but she's got just enough curves in all the right places, her hips flaring slightly, and her little breasts lush and pert.

She looks so fucking ripe it hurts.

And don't even get me started on her lips. Bee-stung and puffy, they're full and pink and have been the star of many of my solo sessions, if you know what I mean. I'm aching to taste them.

And I will.

Soon.

I already have it all planned out.

My heart begins to gallop in my chest in anticipation.

I'm coiled up tighter than a spring.

I can hardly focus thinking about what's to come.

Just one more day, and I can put my plan into action.

New Year's Eve.

———

Lexi

I paste a smile on my face and try to act like I'm genuinely happy to be here with my friend, Marissa, but in all honesty, I wish I was just at home resting.

I love dancing. I do it all day, but the dancing I do after hours at the strip club to put me through dance school is starting to take its toll on me. I'm not getting enough sleep, and my feet are sore and aching.

There was no way Marissa was going to leave me alone on New Year's Eve, though. She wanted to come out to this New Year's Eve bash, and there was no way I could in good conscience send my bestie off to it by herself, so here I am.

Though I'm not sure why I came since my bubbly friend keeps flitting off to flirt and dance with every hot guy she sees.

I'm mostly standing here by myself, sipping some fruity little drink that's non-alcoholic since I'm not technically old enough to drink at only nineteen.

The beat is bumping, and while it's not the flowing lyrical music that I really love to dance to, I find myself swaying my hips to it anyway.

I guess working at the strip club is starting to rub off on me. I'm starting to like more of these hip-hop, modern beats.

I frown down into my glass when I think about where I work. I hate it, but I realize how lucky I am to make the kind of money I make there without ever even having to take off my clothes. I never show more skin than I would if I was wearing a bikini on a beach, and I honestly don't know how I managed to secure that deal from my boss, but I'd been adamant when he'd hired me that I didn't want to actually strip. That I would just dance. I promised him that my dancing alone would be enough to bring in the money, and he'd given me a chance to only dance without actually stripping, stating that if I could deliver, he didn't really give a shit one way or another if I got naked.

And I did. Deliver, that is. I'm his highest-earning girl, though I never even so much as flash a nipple.

I know I'm a good dancer, and that just proves it. If only I could get the break I need to dance on a big stage and not just in a strip joint, though.

I sigh and then scan the crowd for Marissa.

She's in the middle of the dance floor with three men dancing with her.

I mentally roll my eyes. Why the hell did I have to come here anyway? I consider slipping off, but I would feel terrible if she didn't have anyone to take her home. Not like we drove here or anything. We took a taxi, but still. A good friend makes sure her bestie gets home okay—especially when it's obvious said bestie has been partaking in her share of underage drinking.

I glance up at the gigantic clock that's been hung on the wall so all the New Year's partiers can watch the clock tick down to the New Year.

It's just five minutes until midnight.

I'm not the only one who's noticed because the DJ comes over the mic and makes the announcement. He brings everyone's attention to the impending New Year's countdown again when the clock is only one minute from the New Year.

A feeling of excitement is buzzing in

the air, and I take in the festive New Year's hats and masks many people are sporting. The most Marissa and I did to dress up is outfit ourselves in minuscule little dresses that barely cover our asses —courtesy of Marissa's barely there wardrobe, of course.

I self-consciously pull on the hem of my dress, tugging it down yet again.

The music stops as people excitedly begin counting down the New Year.

"Ten! Nine! Eight..." As the count-down continues, a figure materializes before me, almost as if he was conjured out of thin air. That's how stealthily he emerges from the crowd.

I crane my neck up to look at the masked man who's undeniably approaching me.

I can tell from here that he's ripped, his long-sleeved black shirt clinging to every bulge of muscles in his arms and chest that tapers down to what I already know are washboard abs and thighs made of granite.

I drag my eyes up his body to his face. He has a strong, stubbled jawline and dark hair that's haphazardly ruffled in that stylishly sexy way. Eyes like molten chocolate are pinned on me from behind the simple black mask he wears.

I've never seen a more beautiful embodiment of primal male masculinity in all my life.

My breath hitches at the intense way he stares at me, his eyes unwavering as he stalks slowly over to me like a panther cornering its prey.

And I'm like a deer caught in the headlights, mesmerized by him. I can't look away. His eyes are holding me captive, and I can't think—much less move.

I vaguely register the sound of the crowd finishing the countdown. It's like everything is in slow motion. The rest of the world blurs out and there is nothing but me and this man.

And then he's standing before me, towering over me. He's so close I can feel the heat emanating off him, smell his clean, masculine scent, an intoxicating scent that has my head spinning. I feel my cheeks heat, and my heart takes up a staccato rhythm, pulsing in overdrive, though I don't know why he affects me so.

"Three! Two! One!" the crowd roars the final countdown, and people all around us begin kissing, but I barely notice them out of the corner of my eyes because my eyes are locked with the mystery man's.

Very deliberately, the man continues to hold my gaze as he lowers his lips to mine.

And then they're on me, and it's like I've been zapped back to life. I've been dead before this moment, but the electric touch of his lips on mine sends surges of current pulsing throughout my entire body. I feel the buzzing all the way to my fingertips and toes.

He kisses me like I've never been kissed before in my entire life.

His lips press firmly yet insistently against mine as his tongue seeks entry into my mouth.

My mouth opens willingly, and he groans as he slips inside, his arms going around me to gather me to him, and dear god.

He presses me flush against his hard body while his tongue plunders my mouth, mating with mine like he's claiming me.

I feel the swollen ridge of his erection pressing into my stomach through his jeans, and sweet baby Jesus. He's just as huge there as he is everywhere else.

I'm still a virgin, but even I know this man is more well-endowed than the average man.

His hands fist in my hair as he angles my head up to him, holding me how he wants me so he can take what he wants from my mouth.

I whimper as heat pools between my thighs, and I feel the area between my legs start to ache and throb.

I fist my hands in his shirt and hold on to him for dear life to keep from falling. My legs feel shaky—like they could buckle at any minute.

This man has completely ruined me. He's wrecked me with this one kiss.

And when he finally pulls back and

rests his forehead against mine, looking down into my eyes like he adores me, like he's known me forever, all I can do is stare back up at him in a slack-jawed, wide-eyed stupor.

What in the holy fuck?

CHAPTER
Two

Cal

I CAN'T STOP STARING into her eyes. They're bewitching me with their wide-eyed innocence. Oh, my little temptress might dance on a stage and have men salivating all over her, but I know she's untouched. It's in the purity I see every time I look into her eyes. It's in the way she blushes, the way she's trembling in my arms right now.

And fuck me if that doesn't make me even hotter for her. Every cell within my body is screaming at me to take her, claim her as *mine. Mine, mine, mine.*

Whether she realizes it or not, she's already mine. She belongs to me.

I know I've been obsessed with her for a long fucking time now, but that doesn't negate the fact of this current that's pulsing between us like a live wire.

I know I'm not imaging it, and I know she feels it too.

This is real. It's raw. It's truer than any fucking thing I've ever felt in my life.

I can finally breathe again. For months, my chest has been tight, on the verge of exploding, but now that I finally have her held securely in my arms, the tension lightens. I draw in a deep breath, enjoying the way my chest expands, savoring the sweet berry scent of her shampoo.

She smells so goddamned delicious. I want to taste her from head to toe, lap at her like a dog, worship at her feet. She's my goddess, my deity, all I'll ever need from here on out.

I pull the mask from my face, finally allowing her to take in all of me. Her eyes sweep over my visage. I'm ten years older than her, but she doesn't seem to care. Thank fuck because I'm too far gone on her to turn back now.

"Happy New Year," I tell her, my voice coming out gruff.

She continues to stare at me, shocked by being kissed by a complete stranger, but what she doesn't know is we aren't strangers.

Not by any means. I know her better than anyone.

I don't want to scare her, but Jesus Christ, every muscle in my body is taut with the effort it takes me to keep from claiming her right here in front of everyone. I don't give a fuck. I just *need* her so fucking much.

Having the culmination of all my hopes and dreams finally in my arms has me almost dizzy with elation.

"Who are you?" she finally manages to speak, her voice coming out soft and breathy.

It makes my cock harden even more inside my pants.

Hell, everything about her has me hardening.

Her lips are swollen and glistening from our kiss, and I feel a bead of precum leak from my tip at the sight.

I fight back a groan. "I'm Cal," I introduce myself to her.

She studies me another moment before she supplies her own name, "I'm Lexi."

I nod. I already know, but she doesn't need to know that.

She continues to stare up at me. I'm lost in her eyes. This is so fucking deep. I've never felt anything like it.

"Let me take you home," I breathe against her lips, dying to taste her again.

I see a flicker of indecision in her eyes, and my soul panics.

I can't fucking lose her. Not know that I've just got her.

So, I kiss her again. Deeply, desperately, renewing the connection I know she felt at our first kiss.

It works. I feel her melt against me. I

wrap my arms around her triumphantly, holding her tightly against me.

When we finally break away from each other, I look down into her dazed eyes and know I've got her.

"Marissa," she shakes her head and trips over her words. "My friend. I can't just leave her. I need to…"

I nod, letting her know that I understand. I can't stop myself from reaching out and tucking one long lock of red hair behind her ear, stroking gently over her cheek when I'm done. God, she's so fucking soft. "You need to make sure she'll be okay," I supply, finishing her sentence for her while she just stares up at me with those soft green eyes that will be my undoing.

She nods, affirming my statement.

I wrap an arm protectively around her shoulders and let her lead us through the crowd to where her friend is laughing in the center of a group of men.

I do the talking before Lexi gets a chance to say anything. I don't want her to get cold feet and talk herself out of anything. "Do you mind if I steal your friend away for the night?" I ask the bubbly blonde, giving her my most charming smile, already knowing that she's going to say it's okay.

Her eyes widen as she takes me in, and then her eyes flick over to her friend mischievously. "Not at all! Please take her!"

Lexi's cheeks pinken, and I grin. Oh, I plan on taking her. I just wink at her friend before escorting my little dancer out of the club and onto the still pretty crowded but less raucous street.

"Would you like to walk?" I ask her. "My place isn't very far from here, but we can get a cab if you like."

She smiles timidly up at me. "Walking sounds nice."

I take her hand and instantly feel that current running through us. She glances up at me with wide eyes.

Yes, I know little one. You feel it too.

It's just like the first time I saw her up on that stage looking too fucking pretty and dainty to be real. I felt in then, this inexplicable pull to her, and

I've felt it every day since then. That's why I've been silently watching her, keeping guard over her, loving her from afar, waiting, waiting.

Until the time was right.

And now it is.

My eyes trail down over her for the hundredth time this night. Her little black dress is short—too damn short. Shorter than I know she would ever wear on her own, which lets me know it's courtesy of her friend. It shows off her incredible legs, her lithe, shapely little thighs and calves. I'd had my hands full glaring at every motherfucker in the club tonight and warning them away from her so nobody messes with her.

She's mine.

Always mine.

I'll gut anyone who touches her except me.

Maybe I'm a little over the top and insane when it comes to her, but I can't help it.

She's the reason I breathe every minute of the day. My reason for living.

My everything.

And she's fixing to find out just how much I feel for her.

I can't hold it in any longer.

Now that I've kissed her and claimed her in even that smallest way, I'll die without her.

———

Lexi

His place might not be very far from the club, but I seriously overestimated my ability to walk for very long in these stilettos. We haven't even been walking for five minutes, Cal's big hand wrapped securely around mine, before my feet start hurting. I bite my lip, trying not to wince.

He notices, of course, and wordlessly scoops me up into his arms like I weigh nothing.

My cheeks burn as I instinctively wrap my arms around his neck to hold on. "I can walk," I protest weakly.

"What if I just like having you in my

arms?" he crooks an eyebrow at me as he levels me with the intensity of his eyes again.

I lick my lips, unsure of how to answer him, and his eyes hone in on the motion. They darken before they flick back up, capturing my own eyes again.

My breath hitches at the look in his eyes. It's hungry and purposeful, and his footsteps speed up.

We're silent as he carries me the rest of the way to his place. It's not an awkward silence though. It's an antici-patory one. Sexual tension is rolling between us so thick neither one of us can speak.

I know without a shadow of a doubt this is the night I'm going to lose my virginity, and the way my body is sparking every time his eyes come down to rest on me, I suspect it's going to be so much more intense than I ever dreamed it could be.

Part of me can't believe I'm doing this. That I'm letting a man I just met carry me off to his place to sexually seduce me, but then another part of me doesn't really feel like he's a stranger.

I feel at peace in his arms. Safe, secure.

Home.

Is that crazy?

CHAPTER

Three

HE DOESN'T SET me down when he gets to the doorway. Instead, he unlocks the door with one hand while still holding me securely against his chest.

I look up at the building we're standing in front of.

It's a gym. One I've walked past many times on my way to work at the nightclub.

He catches my questioning look and explains, "I own this place. My private loft is upstairs above the gym."

That explains his ripped body then. He probably works out all day every day.

He still doesn't set me down when

he crosses over the threshold and closes the door behind us. He carries me to the back of the building and then up a flight of stairs leading to his loft above the gym.

Only when he closes the door to his loft does he finally set me on my feet.

I take in the expansive space decorated in modern décor. Everything is clean with straight lines. It's a contemporary space, and very masculine in nature.

I don't have much time to glance around, though, because before I know it Cal is on me, pressing my back against the wall, filling my entire line of vision.

He just stands there pressed against me, breathing on me, his lips right against mine. I feel his heart beating against mine, and there's something so intimate about the act of him standing there letting his heart pulse in tune with mine, beating in their own private dance.

"Do you feel that?" he whispers against my lips. "Our hearts beating as one?"

I nod, and he rakes a hand into my hair, a groan tearing from his chest. "You were made for me, Lexi," his voice is husky.

This is so intense. Almost too intense. I'm shaking with emotion, trembling against him. It's a good thing he's got me pressed against the wall because otherwise I'd fall into a heap at his feet. My legs are shaking so badly.

"Say you'll be mine forever," he whispers against my lips. I taste each minty word he breathes onto me.

He doesn't give me a chance to answer him before his lips capture mine. He sucks on my bottom lip, groaning, before he finally dips his tongue into my mouth and skillfully twines it with mine.

God, the man can kiss. Just his kisses alone have me turned into a ball of need. Every nerve in my body is on fire, craving more of him. His kisses steal all thought from my mind. All I can do is press myself as close to him as I can get.

I feel his hands running down my back, along my ass and to my legs, which he hoists up and wraps around him.

And then I feel him, his hard cock pressed right against the apex of my thighs.

I whimper when he begins to cant his hips into me, humping me through our clothes.

Moisture pools between my legs as he keeps grinding against me, creating a delicious friction that has me mewling out his name, "Cal!"

A shudder passes through him when I say his name.

"Fuck," he growls, his voice gravelly, "do you know how fucking crazy it makes me to hear you whimpering my name like that?"

He moves his mouth to my neck and begins to suck hard. I know he's pulling all the blood to the surface and that there will be a hickey left behind. I've always thought they were gross. I never could understand why a girl would let a guy do that to her, but the way he is sucking on me like I'm a ripe persimmon that he's trying to devour, I completely understand.

His lips and tongue feel like heaven. I'm willing to let him put how ever many marks on me he wants. And I'll wear them with pride.

As if he can read my thoughts, he rasps, "Gonna make sure everyone knows who you belong to. From this moment on, you'll always wear my mark, baby."

I don't argue with him. Maybe his possessive words so shortly after we just met should alarm me, but they don't.

On the contrary, they settle deep within my soul, warming me, making me feel desired and wanted, filling me with a rush of feminine power that I can make this big, gorgeous man lose control like this.

The next thing I know, he's yanking down the top of my dress, exposing my breasts. He makes a strangled noise as he looks at them.

I flush but not with embarrassment. This man's reaction to me is setting me aflame. The sounds he makes are turning me on just as much as his kisses and touches.

It's like he's enthralled by me—everything about me—and that does something to me. It makes me all warm and tingly inside and gives me a heady rush.

His hot tongue flicks out to swirl across one nipple while he palms my other breast, his hand completely covering it as he tests its weight in his hand.

My hands move of their own volition to fist in his hair when he begins to suckle on my nipple.

My panties are sopping wet now, and he finds that out when he finally reaches under my dress and rubs his fingers over me through them.

He hisses in a breath. "That little pussy is weeping for me, isn't it, honey?"

He reaches down to unzip his pants. His cock springs forward and slaps my thigh, and I feel it dripping precum onto my skin. "It's okay. My body weeps for you too, sweetheart," he rasps as if he's in pain.

I reach down and wrap my fingers around him, marveling at the velvety feel of his hardness. His girth is so big I can't even wrap my fingers all the way around him, and my eyes widen even as my core pulses. I want this. I want him, but dear lord, he's going to split me in half. There's no way he'll fit.

"Christ," he croaks out as he rips my panties clean off me. "I can't fucking wait, honey. I've got to be inside you *now*."

He lines his fat tip up with my hole and holds onto my ass as he begins to press up into me.

My mouth opens in a silent "o" as I feel him stretching me.

His eyes never leave mine as he pushes slowly yet steadily up into me.

I begin to whimper the deeper he gets. Oh god, there's no way I'll ever be able to take all of him. I feel so full. More stretched than I ever imagined I could be.

I close my eyes and my head falls

back as I gasp out little panting breaths, trying to calm my erratically beating heart.

"Eyes on me, little Lexi," he commands me, and I snap my eyes open to find his brown orbs blaring into mine.

His own chest is puffing up and down as he breathes in deeply, his nostrils flared with the effort of holding himself back. The evidence of how badly he wants me causes more moisture to flood between my legs, and he slides in further.

We both groan in unison.

Just when I think he's all the way in and start to relax, his eyes go wild, and he bites his lip. "Fuck, Lexi, you're mine!" he roars out before he suddenly slams up into me, burying himself in me to the hilt.

I feel something give way inside me as I scream at the sting, and I realize that he's just broken my hymen.

I'm clinging to him, shaking while he strokes my hair and sits still inside me, unmoving as he tries to soothe me.

As the pain fades, it begins to be

replaced by this deep pressure. I'm aching, and I can feel him pulsing inside me. I involuntarily squeeze my muscles around his throbbing length, and he groans a sound of intense male pleasure.

"Oh fuck, you're strangling my cock, baby," he groans out before he kisses me deeply, desperately.

I kiss him back, my arousal building at the expert way he twines his tongue with mine.

He begins to move inside me while still dancing his tongue with mine.

I moan into his mouth as pleasure snaps along my nerve endings. I'm buzzing, my whole body feeling more alive than it's ever felt.

He presses me deeper into the wall as he picks up the pace and begins to slam into me over and over again. He's so big where I'm small. I'm completely consumed by him.

He finally breaks our kiss in favor of looking down into my eyes. His brown eyes are smoldering down at me, his mouth slightly parted as he humps up into me, pistoning his cock in and out of me.

"This pussy is mine, isn't it, Lexi?" he asks me.

I don't answer. I just throw my head back and moan.

"Huh?" he prompts me. "Say it. Tell me you're mine," he demands.

I still don't speak, too busy chasing the sensations he's giving me. Some-thing is building deep inside me, and I can't talk. All I can do is focus on it. It's building…building…

He slows his pumps, and it begins fading.

I whimper in frustration and look up at him frantically.

"I'll give this little pussy whatever it needs. Any time. Day or night. So long as you tell me you're mine, baby," his voice is pleading and still strained from his exertion. I can't deny him. Or myself.

"I'm yours!" I scream.

He immediately rewards me with several hard jabs.

"Damn right you are," he grates out in between thrusts.

"You love that big cock splitting you in half, baby?" He's speaking right into my ear. Something coils tightly in my stomach at his words. His voice, his words have me just as mesmerized as the rest of him.

"Uh-huh," I manage to moan out, not wanting him to stop again.

"Good because it's the only one you're ever going to have up inside that sweet cunt."

He pulls back to look down between us where his cock is glistening with my juices. "Look at that," he marvels. "You take me so well, honey. That pussy was made for me to fuck. Made for me to bust a big load in."

I begin to ripple as he continues to spew filth in my ear.

He feels it, and it spurs him on. "You like that, don't you, sexy little Lexi? You like knowing that you got me fixing to nut all up in that sweet little pussy. Yeah, you do." He lets out a grunt as he continues to saw into me. "Well, you're fixing to make me come, little girl. Let me feel that little thing fall open all around me. Come on my cock if you want that nut, baby."

He moves his hand down between us and begins to rub my clit. "Oh my god!" I groan out, my head falling back against the wall.

"Eyes," he snaps. "Look at me. I want to see you when you come for me."

I look at him frantically. "Cal!" I call out, half sobbing, half pleading.

"That's right. Say my name when you come on my dick." He jabs up inside me one last time and smashes down on my clit.

I scream.

My entire body spasms, and my vision goes white. I literally see fucking stars.

When I come back, I see his brown eyes staring right at me lustfully, adoringly, before he bellows and holds himself deep inside my tunnel.

I feel him emptying himself deep within me. Spray after spray of heat jets up into my womb. He's pulsing and jerking inside me. His mouth is parted in wonder, and his eyes never leave mine as he gives me everything he's got.

When he's done, he slouches forward slightly, holding us against the wall, his still hard cock still pulsing within me.

He kisses my eyes and then my cheeks before taking my mouth in a one-lip kiss so tender I feel like my heart is going to burst.

"Please tell me I can keep you," he pleads against my lips. "I know you can feel this. You feel that you're mine, don't you?"

I don't know what to say, so I just nod against his chest and wrap my arms around him as I burrow my face in the crook of his neck.

It feels so right here in his arms.

Still inside me, he carries us to his bed and lays us down on it.

He strokes my face and just stares down at me wonderingly, and I stare back up at him. This super intense man who's claimed me in more ways than one tonight.

I close my eyes and nuzzle into his chest, exhaustion overtaking me.

I still feel his hands stroking all over my body, petting me gently as I drift off in his arms.

CHAPTER
Four

Lexi

I DON'T KNOW how long I sleep, but when I awaken, I'm all alone in Cal's huge bed.

I'm naked, so he must have undressed me at some point. My dress is nowhere to be found, so I get up and go over to his closet.

I find a black hoodie and slip it on over my head. It dwarfs me, coming down to my knees, the sleeves falling down to cover my hands.

It smells like Cal, though, and I wrap

my arms about myself, inhaling deeply and softly smiling to myself.

I pad out of the bedroom and begin walking softly from room to room, searching for him.

I come across a closed door and slowly open it, peeking inside.

My breath catches, and I push the door all the way open when I see pictures taped up all over the wall.

My heart begins to drum within my chest as I step into the room and look around incredulously.

It's not a very big space. It's probably the smallest room in the loft, but every square inch of the walls is covered.

With pictures.

Of *me*.

My arms and legs feel numb as I walk in a circle around the room, seeing myself in various candids. I'm walking down the street in some. I'm dancing at the nightclub in others. I'm even sitting in my apartment in some.

Oh. My. God.

Cal has been stalking me.

For months it looks like.

This entire room is a shrine to me, detailing just how deep his obsession goes.

Suddenly it all makes sense. Him begging me to tell him I was his, all the possessive talk.

How long has he been planning all this?

Icy fingers prick my neck, and I turn around to find him standing in the doorway.

He's wearing a pair of sweatpants but no shirt, and I gape at what I see.

My name is tattooed into his chest right over his heart.

He begins walking slowly toward me, his expression one of caution like he thinks I'm a frightened animal that's about to bolt on him.

That's not far from the truth.

For every step he takes forward, I take a step back. I realize that I'm trapping myself deeper within the room, but I'm acting on instinct.

He holds his hands up in supplication. "Lexi." All he says is my name, but it's enough to open up the floodgates.

"How long have you been stalking me?" My voice is shaking with betrayal.

"Ever since I first laid eyes on you," he admits. "I knew, I fucking knew, you were made to be mine." His voice sounds tortured, begging me to understand. "I know you feel it too. I know you felt our connection tonight."

I can't deny that. I did. I do. I still feel connected to him, but I can't be okay with him stalking me.

Can I?

I shake my head. "This isn't right."

His face betrays his hurt. He stops like I punched him. "Don't fucking say that," his voice is a low growl. "Don't you dare try to talk yourself out of this. Don't run away from me. You already told me you were mine, Lexi." His jaw hardens with his last statement, and I feel a moment of alarm.

Would he keep me here against my will?

I don't wait to find out.

My eyes flick to the door, and then I sprint, hurling past him as fast as my legs will carry me.

"Lexi!" he calls out from behind me.

Something in his broken voices rips at my heart and tells me to stop! To turn around and run back to him, that none of it matters except how we feel.

But then there's that other part that's been ingrained in me by society, that part that tells me this isn't normal and that I need to run far away.

I listen to the second part and keep running. I run out of his building and take off down the darkened streets.

I know that I can't be too fast for him. Even though he's huge, he's in a great shape. I know he could catch me in a minute if he really wanted to, so I finally calm down enough to walk. I glance back over my shoulder, but I don't see him. He must have let me go.

For now, anyway.

I begin chewing on my lip as my thoughts clash within my head. I don't know where I'm going. I'm just walking aimlessly, thinking.

I can't go back to my place. He knows where I live. He'll find me there.

I think back on how gentle he was

when he kissed me, the adoration in his eyes. Surely, if he meant me harm, he wouldn't have held me so tenderly.

Then, I remember the intensity in his eyes, his possessive words claiming I was his, that I belonged to him. I remember the feeling of him slamming up inside me, the almost violent way he marked me. Maybe that should instill fear in me, but it doesn't.

Instead, I shudder in pleasure at the memory. I loved his ferociousness, the way he made me feel so wanted.

My footsteps slow. Maybe he is obsessed with me, but is that really so bad? Somehow I know deep down in my soul that he'd never hurt me, that he's been secretly watching over me all this time. I think back on how no one from the strip club ever bothered me, and I suddenly know with absolute certainty that it wasn't because I was lucky or the universe was somehow protecting me.

It was because of him.

Cal. It's Cal who's been silently protecting me.

Watching over me from afar.

Warmth suddenly floods through me when I think of how much he must truly feel for me to do that.

I don't understand why he didn't approach me sooner. Why he stalked me and waited so long, but it doesn't even matter.

He's right. We do have a connection. I felt it in that first kiss tonight, that kiss that brought my New Year in with a bang and irrevocably changed my life forever.

I stop walking entirely. I don't know what this is. It's probably crazy. Maybe he's crazy. Maybe I'm crazy. Maybe *we're* crazy, but I suddenly know what I have to do.

I have to return to him.

I swallow and look around me. The only problem is I don't know where I've wandered to. I was so lost in my thoughts I didn't pay any attention to where I was going.

And I suddenly realize that I'm still just wearing Cal's hoodie when two men step out of the shadows and begin sizing me up with dangerous gleams in their eyes.

I don't even take the time to scream.

I just pivot on my heels and run again.

Only this time, I'm running back to my stalker and not away from him.

CHAPTER
Five

Cal

I SEE the moment Lexi decides to come back to me. I know every expression on her face by heart. I can read her thoughts without her ever voicing them. I've studied her for so long there's nothing she can hide from me.

That's how I knew she was going to run from me earlier when she saw my shrine to her—in both my home and on my chest. I knew she'd have to see everything eventually, but I hadn't meant for her to get so frightened yet. I was hoping to wait until I had more time to ease her into it.

I watched her sleep for the longest time. The way her eyelashes lay on her porcelain cheeks. The way her little, rosy lips bowed slightly in her slumber.

I could have watched her all night, but I got up to check the gym and make sure I'd locked everything up when I carried her in earlier that night. I'd been so drunk with lust with her in my arms I couldn't think straight, much less remember if I'd locked up like I should have.

By the time I'd come back, she'd stumbled upon everything.

My heart had wrenched within my chest at the look on her face even as I'd felt a primal surge of satisfaction seeing her swaddled in my clothing.

My chest aches at the thought of losing her.

I can't bear it.

Now that I've had her, I can't bear to lose her.

I'll blow my brains out.

But I can't do that because I can't leave her all alone. Unprotected.

I didn't know what to do when she ran from me. Against my every instinct I let her go, gave her space, internally praying to whatever deity out there was listening that she would return to me.

But, of course, I couldn't leave her on these streets alone.

So, I followed her. Once again, silently watching her, worshipping her from afar.

And thank fuck I did because when I see two men step out from the shadows and leer down at her, an inhuman roar bubbles up in my chest.

My vision goes red as rage like I've never known overtakes me when I see the stark fear in her eyes as she turns and begins running away from them.

"Lexi!" I scream at her from across the street before I sail over the pavement, crossing the street to her as fast as my legs will carry me.

Her head turns toward me, and she changes direction, barreling to me.

"Cal!" she sobs out as she flings herself into my arms.

I catch her, holding her tightly against my chest as she wraps her arms and legs around me like a little chimp.

The men see me and the murderous look on my face. They stop in their tracks and look at one another before they begin mumbling and turn around, deciding that Lexi's not worth the trouble of going through me.

They're damn fucking lucky she's here in my arms or their blood would be splattered on this sidewalk right now.

She's trembling like a little leaf against me, and I run my hands over her, hating the feeling of her being scared. "Sshh, I've got you, baby. They're gone now. No one's ever going to hurt you. I fucking swear it to you." I've never meant anything more in my fucking life either. I'd die to protect her.

She pulls back and hazards a glance over her shoulder, checking to make sure they really are gone. When she turns back to me, her eyes are tear-stained. "I'm so sorry, Cal," she tells me. "I shouldn't have run from you."

I cup her cheek, marveling at how her entire cheek fits within my big palm. She's so tiny, and yet we somehow fit. She fits perfectly in my arms, against my body, her curves molding to me like a missing puzzle piece.

I give an incredulous laugh. I can't believe this sweet angel is apologizing to me. She's done nothing wrong. In fact, her reaction was completely warranted. I'm the demented fuck. Not her. "I'm sorry you had to find out the way you did. I was going to tell you. I just wanted more time with you first." My voice is strained with my next confession. "I fucking love you, Lexi. I've loved you from the moment I set eyes on you. I'm obsessed you. You're my everything. If you truly knew how long, you'd probably run from me all over again."

I feel gutted, flayed open at the thought, and I do nothing to try to hide my despair at that thought.

Her eyes soften. "It did scare me at

first, I'll admit." She stops talking to worry her lips between her teeth as she thinks. I fight back a groan, wanting to take that lip in between my own teeth. She finally releases it, leaving it pink and swollen in the wake of her ministrations before she goes on, "But somehow I know you would never hurt me."

"Never," I vow, pulling her closer to me. "I'll kill anyone who does."

She cocks her head to the side questioningly. "But I do want to know why? Why did you stalk me for so long and not approach me sooner?"

I exhale a breath. "I don't know, baby. Because I'm so much older than you maybe?"

She frowns. "How old are you? You don't look old."

I throw my head back and laugh before I tell her, "I'm twenty-nine."

She shrugs, "That's only ten years."

I shake my head before I continue with my reasoning, "There you were this beautiful young dancer. I was scared to approach you. I happened to see you in that bar, and I didn't want you to think I was like all those other dudes, just wanting to fuck you."

My eyes take on a faraway look as I recount the memory. I can still see it all so clearly in my mind's eyes. "I saw you, and it's like I couldn't fucking breathe without seeing you again."

I look down at her, begging with her to understand. "I had to watch you. I had to see you every day, or I felt like I was going to die. I've never in my life had anything like you happen to me."

"I'm not some sick stalker type. Just with you, baby. I'll admit I'm more than a little obsessed you, but it's just you. Only you. I didn't approach you because I didn't know what the fuck I would do if you turned me down. It'd crush me. I wouldn't be able to handle it. So, I watched you instead, got to know you and then approached you in a way I thought you couldn't say no to."

She's staring up at me thoughtfully. "I think I understand now," she says slowly.

Relief floods my chest, and I drop my forehead to hers, staring into her eyes, needing to feel our connection. "So, you'll let me keep you?" I ask her, acting like I'm giving her a choice. I pray with everything in me she says yes because if she doesn't I just might chain her up with me anyway. I'm that far gone for her.

"Yes," she whispers against my lips before she tilts her lips up and kisses me.

I kiss her with all the love and obsession in my heart for her.

"Happy New Year," she finally whispers my words from our first kiss back to me, and I smile against her lips.

"Best way I've ever brought in the New Year," I tell her honestly before kissing her again.

My love. My Lexi.

My obsession.

Epilogue

One Year Later

Cal

I'M SITTING in the front row like I do at every performance my wife gives.

She finally got the break she was looking for. She's been noticed, and she's headlining dance performances left and right.

Like I always knew she would be. My little flower is amazing.

I'm so fucking proud of her I could burst.

She's beautiful up there in the spotlight. Poetry in motion, her body swaying gently, gracefully. I can't look away from her.

I could watch her flit around on that stage like a little butterfly every second of the day.

Lexi and I didn't waste any time getting married. I was so anxious to have her belong to me in every way, we got married on New Year's Day. Some people might say it was sudden, but we knew our hearts.

Nothing about how our relationship began was conventional, but fuck what the world says.

All that matters is us.

At my insistence, she stopped working at the nightclub immediately. She was more than happy to oblige. She hated working there. I pay for her schooling and anything else she needs.

She's mine.

Mine to love. Mine to care for. Mine to spoil.

Mine to fuck.

My dick hardens in my pants as I

watch her leap into the air, her red hair flowing out around her like flames. A goddess, my woman.

Every fucking thing she does turns me on.

I can't wait to get her alone.

Breed her. My chest tightens. The need to put my seed in her is so strong I can hardly think straight.

I want everything with Lexi. Kids, family, the whole she-bang.

But I know her dancing is important to her, and she was just put on the map. I can't be selfish and take that away from her, so we compromised. We'll have kids someday in the future. Right now she's going to focus on her dance.

As much as I hate her little birth control pills, I allow them. I'm not going to lie. I've been tempted to throw the fuckers out. It pisses me off to no end to know that they're blocking my seed from taking root in her fertile womb and doing what it's supposed to do.

The birth control pills were a compromise too. I balked when she suggested condoms. No way was I going to have anything between us.

Never.

Not even a rubber.

I want us to be as close as possible. Always. Skin on skin. Her soul joined to mine.

I'm still just as obsessed with her as always. Maybe even more so, though I've tried to cut back on my stalking.

I've taken on more personal training sessions to keep myself busy while she's training, though I still obsessively check my phone every five minutes to make sure I can see where she's at on the tracking app I have, which she of course knows about and is okay with.

She knows I can't breathe if I don't know where she's at every minute of the day.

Maybe I'm a controlling bastard, but she loves me anyway, and we're okay with us so fuck everyone else.

The audience leaps to their feet, applauding her raucously. I'm right there with them, cheering louder for her than anyone else in the audience.

Her eyes immediately find mine, and she smiles that special smile I know is just for me.

My god, if she asked me to rip my heart out and hand it to her, I'd do it.

I'd do anything for her.

I rush backstage, eager to greet her.

When she comes into her dressing room, I'm already there waiting for her.

I close the door behind her, locking it. Her eyes widen, and her little tongue darts out to wet her lips. She already knows what's going to happen.

I sit down on the little settee and pull her into my lap so she's straddling me.

"Fuck, honey, I can't wait," I growl at her as I tear at her leotard, ripping it clean from her body.

She doesn't even gasp. She's used to me ripping her clothes from her. She's got a hundred pairs of backups because she knows after almost every performance, I'm so damn hard up for her I can't see straight until I wet my dick in her.

"It feels like somebody liked my performance," she teases me as she wiggles on my lap, dragging her sweet cunt up and down my length through my pants.

I waste no time in releasing my cock. It swells up out of my fly as I unzip, the head swollen and leaking. "Of course I did. You know I can't take watching you up there twirling around, those perfect little thighs mesmerizing me, wishing they were wrapped around my waist."

She moans and drags her dripping wet hole up and down my dick.

I throw my head back and groan. Jesus Christ. She drives me crazy. "You keep doing that I'm going to bust before I ever make it inside your pussy."

"Oh god," she cries out when I shift under her and grab her hips, yanking her down onto me, impaling her onto my swollen length.

A moan tears up out of my chest, and my eyes damn near roll back in my head at how tight she is.

"Mine," I grit out as I begin to hammer up into her.

"Yours," she agrees with me as she

bounces up and down on my cock, her face flushed prettily.

She looks so goddamned beautiful riding my cock.

I lean forward and suck the peaks of her nipples through the thin material covering her chest. She arches into my mouth on a whine, moisture flooding my cock as she begins to come.

I fuck her through her orgasm, feeling my own release building in me.

My balls tighten up, and I yank her head down to mine, thrusting my tongue in her mouth, wanting to taste her as I spend inside her.

My tongue mates with hers frantically as I pump up into her in a series of untimed jerks.

Fuuuuuck.

She whimpers under the assault, and then I feel her spasming around me again.

She screams into my mouth as her second orgasm hits her, and the feeling of her falling apart on me again tips me over the edge.

I shoot my load up into her. My cum

rips out of my cock violently, the intensity of my own orgasm damn near taking my breath away. I come so hard it almost makes me dizzy, filling her up to the brim like I always do.

She's lax in my arms, laying against me limply like a ragdoll.

"Good thing you're on birth control or I think that load would have definitely gotten you pregnant," I chuckle into her hair, a prick of wistfulness overtaking me. One day, I remind myself. She'll swell with my child one day.

She pulls back and looks down between us, biting her lip, before she finally drags her eyes up to mine. "I'm not on birth control anymore, Cal," she admits conspiratorially. "I came off it this morning."

I go completely still as I process the implication of her words. "You're not?" I ask her slowly, incredulously. "But, honey, what about your career? Your dancing?" I search her eyes, but my heart is starting to hammer within my chest as hope buoys me.

She shakes her little head with a

smile, her flaming curls bouncing so prettily I want to kiss her again. "I spoke to the director. He assured me I could always come back to the stage any time I want. Besides, even if I couldn't, *we're* more important to us. Starting a family. A little piece of me and you." She lays her hand on her stomach like she's already pregnant, and I cover her hand with my own, my heart soaring at her words.

I kiss her again, pouring everything I can't put into words into our connection, and the way she wraps her arms around me and kisses me back lets me know that she hears me loud and clear.

"You're perfect. You know that?" I tell her, my voice rough with emotion.

I don't deserve her, but I'm going to do every damn thing within my power to make sure she's safe and happy for the rest of our lives.

"I love you, Cal," she whispers against my lips before kissing me again.

Those words never fail to tighten my chest with emotion.

Mine. She's all mine.

THE END

Connect with Emma!

Visit Emma's website to get a FREE book you can't get anywhere else: www.authoremmabray.com.

www.ingramcontent.com/pod-product-compliance
Lightning Source LLC
Chambersburg PA
CBHW031133160726
47989CB00017B/2904